A Trailblazer Curriculum Guide

JULIA PFERDEHIRT

WITH DAVE & NETA JACKSON

BETHANY HOUSE PUBLISHERS
MINNEAPOLIS, MINNESOTA 55438

CONTENTS

Published by Bethany House Publishers
A Ministry of Bethany Fellowship International
11400 Hampshire Ave. South
Minneapolis, Minnesota 55438
www.bethanyhouse.com
ISBN 0-7642-2344-5
Printed in the United States of America by
Bethany Press International, Minneapolis, Minnesota 55438

HOW TO USE THIS GUIDE

Welcome to the TRAILBLAZER BOOKS Curriculum Guides! As a teacher or homeschooling parent, you're glad when you see your students with their noses in books. But a good story is only the beginning of a learning adventure. Since the TRAILBLAZER BOOKS take readers all over the world into different cultures and time periods, each book opens a door to an exciting, humanities-based study that includes geography, history, social studies, literature, and language arts.

This Curriculum Guide for *Shanghaied to China* about Hudson Taylor puts a host of activities and resources at your fingertips to help launch your students on a journey of discovery. The wealth of options allows you to choose the best pace and content for your students. You might want to assign students to simply read the book and then do one or two projects on folklore or food, travel or topography. Or you can delve deeper, planning a two-week unit with daily reading and vocabulary, research, creative writing, and hands-on projects. *Advance planning is key to effective use of this guide.*

SCOPE AND SEQUENCE

This guide includes **seven lessons**, enough for a two-week unit. The first and last lessons cover one chapter and provide historical background; all other lessons cover two chapters. All lessons include vocabulary, background information, discussion questions, and suggested activities. **Activities** are grouped by subject matter in the back of this guide: Geography (GEO), History (HIS), Social Studies and Folkways (SS/FW), and Literature and Language Arts (LIT/LA). Within each subject, look for symbols indicating different types of activities (writing, research, speech, reading, hands-on projects, video). Activities and resources particularly appropriate for younger or older students are designated as follows: younger (*), older (**). A three- to five-day Mega Project is also included. All activities list resources and materials needed.

PLANNING

Four to six weeks prior to the study . . .

- Skim *Shanghaied to China*, review lessons

(pages 4–10), and choose activities, noting materials needed.

- Reserve materials on interlibrary loan and order films from specialty sources (titles and authors are listed in the Activities sections; full publication information is available under **Resources** on page 23 of this guide).
- Purchase craft materials.

If you are planning a two-week unit . . .

- Students will cover one lesson daily for seven days.
- Choose one or more short, focused activities to accompany each lesson. Activities especially appropriate to the chapter(s) covered are noted on each lesson page.
- The remaining days can be devoted to the Mega Project found on page 21.

Note: Choose activities based on the age level, interests, and learning needs of your student(s). You might choose one activity from each discipline during the unit, *or* you might opt to balance the different types of activities.

LESSONS

- Assign relevant chapters in *Shanghaied to China* the day before the lesson, to be read either individually *or* out loud as a family.
- **Praise and Prayer**, written by TRAILBLAZER authors Dave and Neta Jackson, provides an opportunity for students to spend a short time in God's Word and apply Scriptural concepts to their own lives.
- Read aloud the **Background** segment, then discuss **Vocabulary and Concepts.** (*Or* ask students to use context clues and a dictionary to define unfamiliar words as they read, leaving puzzling words or concepts to discuss the following day.)
- Give students an opportunity to discuss thoughts and reactions to their reading using the questions in the **Talk About It** feature. Discussion, debate, and interaction can be lively. Enjoy!
- Use the suggested **Activities** or one of your own choosing.

Note: Unless marked otherwise, page and chapter numbers refer to Dave and Neta Jackson's original TRAILBLAZER BOOK *Shanghaied to China*.

HISTORICAL SUMMARY

When Hudson Taylor arrived in Shanghai, China, on March 1, 1854, he stepped into the middle of a three-sided war. He wrote, "A band of rebels known as the Red Turbans had taken possession of the Native City [surrounded by] the imperial army of [40,000] to 50,000 men." These rebels were associated with the Taiping Rebellion that had begun a couple years earlier when Hong Xiuquan organized the peasants to overthrow their harsh rulers. The imperial army represented the Chinese government.

However, in addition to trying to put down an internal rebellion, the Chinese government was also fighting Europeans, especially England, in a confrontation called the Opium Wars.

Hudson Taylor was shocked to discover that his own British government was responsible for importing opium from India and selling it to the Chinese people! People who smoked opium soon became addicts. They didn't care if their families were hungry or their businesses went bankrupt. They lived in a hazy dream world until they died of starvation or disease.

The Chinese government tried to stop the opium trade, outlawing the sale of opium and blocking harbors to keep out the British ships. But selling drugs was making the British rich, so the British and other European governments took military control of the European sections of Chinese cities. They set up their own courts and police, declaring that European people did not have to obey Chinese law. England also sent warships to protect the opium shipments, and because the British ships and weapons were superior to those of the Chinese, the Chinese couldn't stop them.

Hudson Taylor was caught in the middle of these battles. He hated to see poor peasants oppressed by their harsh rulers, so he was sometimes thought to be siding with the Taiping rebels. He also condemned his own country for destroying the lives of so many Chinese people with opium. And he did not want to live separated from the Chinese people in the European section of the city. The British criticized him, and even some fellow missionaries thought he was foolish for living, eating, and dressing like the "idol-worshiping" Chinese!

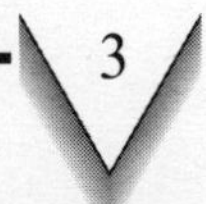

Lesson One

Chapter 1: Knocked on the Head

PRAISE AND PRAYER: UNWILLING SEA PASSENGERS

In *Shanghaied to China*, Neil Thompson ended up "going to sea" unwillingly. The Bible tells about some other unwilling sea passengers. **Read Jonah 1:1–3, 15–17 and Acts 26:32–27:2, 9–12.** Why was the prophet Jonah on a ship? Where did he end up "traveling" for three days and nights? Why was the apostle Paul on a ship? What was the difference between the two men?

Thought: We can't run away or be taken away from God (see Psalm 139:8–12).

Prayer: Thank you, God, that you are with me all day, all night, no matter what I do or where I go. Even when I'm disobedient—you never leave me.

VOCABULARY AND CONCEPTS

Check the resource list for books about sailing ships and nautical terms. The following words may be new to readers: shanghaied, gangplank, stowaway, poop deck, forecastle, port bow, sauntered.

BACKGROUND

In the 1850s, England was a great power on the oceans. England controlled colonies around the globe. These countries were owned and run by England. English merchants made fortunes by shipping and selling goods and natural resources from the colonies in Europe and America. England would have liked to have had China as a colony.

British merchant ships traded goods all over the world. Ships like the *Dumfries* might take manufactured goods from England *to* China and return loaded with tea, silk, or spices. Many British ships were drug runners, picking up opium from the colony of India to sell in China.

. . . so I climbed on top of a barrel to watch.

TALK ABOUT IT

Read the historical summary. Knowing about the opium trade and how Europeans kept themselves separate from the Chinese (even refusing to obey their laws), you can easily figure out what Chinese people might have thought of Europeans. In what ways do you think the reputation of Europeans might have affected Hudson Taylor's ability to tell the Chinese people about Jesus?

INTRODUCTORY ACTIVITY

On your globe or atlas map find Liverpool, England. Trace the journey of the *Dumfries* through the Irish Channel, past Holyhead, past the coast of West Africa, around the Cape of Good Hope, through the South Indian Ocean, passing Australia, Indonesia, and the Palau Islands to the Shanghai harbor.

Lesson Two

Chapter 2: The Fearsome Light on Holyhead
Chapter 3: High Above the Sea

PRAISE AND PRAYER: SHELTERED IN THE STORM

Read Jonah 1:4–2:10 and Acts 27:13–44. How do these storms compare to the storm described in chapters 2 and 3 of *Shanghaied to China*? In each case, how did the people respond? What happened? (On page 27 of *Shanghaied*, Neil tells how waves "thundered down onto our deck one right after the other, filling it full to the bulwarks with sea water." **Find Martin Luther's song "A Might Fortress" in a hymnal.** Why does he call God a "bulwark"? How is God a bulwark?)

Thought: We can ask God for His protection during "storms" in our life.

Prayer: Thank you, Almighty God, that you hear our prayers in the midst of stormy times in our lives.

VOCABULARY AND CONCEPTS

Check the resource list for books about sailing ships from the 1800s and try these nautical terms on for size: steward, royals, yards, spanker, masts, galley, jib, mizzenmast, boom, starboard, port, reef the topsails, bulwarks, forecastle, boatswain.

See pages 19 and 20: Can you figure out what is meant by "getting your sea legs"? Also see page 33: What is a proverb?

. . . as much sail was set as the *Dumfries* could tolerate in such a gale.

BACKGROUND

England, Portugal, France, Holland, and Spain were among the countries that created large companies for trade. England, for example, shipped wool and manufactured goods from English factories to Asia, India, Australia, and Africa. They returned with natural resources like gold and diamonds from Africa or wood for furniture from Indonesian islands. The traders bought teas that could not be grown in England, or interesting spices, cloth, and artwork. Until slavery was outlawed in England in 1833, hundreds of British ships carried kidnapped Africans to be sold as slaves in America.

See *From Slave Ship to Freedom Road* by Julius Lester to learn about the slave trade. Look up *The Old China Trade* by Francis Ross Carpenter about trade with China in the 1700s and 1800s. This book also tells about the Opium Wars.

TALK ABOUT IT

Why do you think it was so important for sailors to be kept busy almost all the time? Recall times and places where squabbles have occurred in your family because people were bored.

ACTIVITIES

LIT/LA 1, 2

Lesson Three

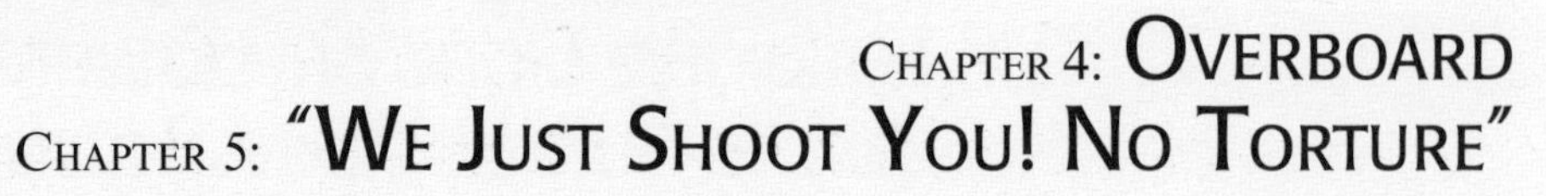

Chapter 4: Overboard
Chapter 5: "We Just Shoot You! No Torture"

PRAISE AND PRAYER: TRUE BEAUTY

All cultures have their own concepts of beauty. In China, binding women's feet was considered beautiful. But what does the Bible have to say about "true beauty"? **Read 1 Peter 3:3–4. Then compare Esther 2:5–7, 17–18 to Esther 4:1–16**. If asked to describe Queen Esther, what would you say were her most important qualities?

Thought: Our inner character is more important to God than outward looks.

Prayer: Dear Lord, help me to develop character qualities that make me a truly beautiful person.

VOCABULARY AND CONCEPTS

reefs, junks, barges, coolies, starboard

"Dropped anchor" on page 49 is a nautical term. What does it mean?

See the historical summary on page 3 of this guide to understand why Neil found the City of Shanghai divided into Chinese and European sections.

I turned to see a smiling Chinese girl just about my age.

BACKGROUND

Many Chinese women's feet were bound to make them "beautiful," but it also made them unable to walk any distance, causing them to be dependent and unable to support themselves. The painful foot binding custom involved breaking bones in the feet to prevent them from growing. It began when girls were toddlers.

The Red Turbans Jeffries mentions on page 51 were probably only one of many rebel groups (see page 3 of this guide).

TALK ABOUT IT

In Chinese culture, bound feet were beautiful. But it painfully limited women's life choices. Think of other foolish "beauty" traditions.

(*Note*: Women once wore so many petticoats and corsets laced so tightly that they could not run, climb stairs easily, engage in sports, and were often ill. Today, very high heels may be "beautiful," but they sometimes damage feet. In some Islamic countries women must wear hot, heavy *chadors* that cover everything but their hands and faces—sometimes only eyes are visible. Some men go hatless in winter because they think wearing hats is not manly.)

Why do you think customs like these develop?

"Public transportation" in Shanghai was rarely by horse-drawn carriage. Usually people rode in carts or chairs pulled or carried by "coolies." Why do you think this hard job was done by people instead of horses?

ACTIVITIES

GEO 1; SS/FW 1

Lesson Four

Chapter 6: The Wreck of the Good Ship *Dumfries*
Chapter 7: Bound Feet and Sky Rockets

PRAISE AND PRAYER: IN THE BOAT WITH JESUS

Look at the last two paragraphs on page 83 of *Shanghaied to China*. **Then read Mark 4:1–2.** Why did Hudson Taylor and Jesus get into small fishing boats? What kind of people listened to them? In what ways was Hudson Taylor "being like Jesus"?

Thought: Not everyone comes to church. If we want to share the Good News about God, we have to go where the people are.

Prayer: Dear Lord, help me to be willing to "get my feet wet" and "get in the boat" so that more people can learn about you.

VOCABULARY AND CONCEPTS

blackball, singsong, civilians, conch shells, mediate, barge, rubble

See page 74. What does Hudson Taylor mean by saying the kind of clothing one wears is not a moral issue?

BACKGROUND

England was a worldwide power on the oceans in 1854. The British merchant ships traded goods on every continent. Huge companies were formed with many great schooner ships. The *Dumfries*, the ship that brought Hudson Taylor to China, was a real ship owned by Aiken and Company out of Liverpool.

British trading companies also brought opium to China. Opium is an addictive drug that eventually kills people who use it. British merchants became wealthy selling opium. When the Chinese government tried to block harbors to stop opium shipments, England's queen sent warships to make sure the opium was delivered. The battles that resulted were called the Opium Wars.

It was Hudson Taylor, . . . dressed for all the world like a Chinese man.

TALK ABOUT IT

On pages 79 and 80, Neil and Mr. Taylor talk about foot binding.

Some people think Americans and other Western people should respect and not judge the traditions of other cultures and people. In fact, Hudson Taylor wore long robes and pointed-toed shoes and even wore his hair in a long braid to show how much he respected Chinese culture and traditions! But Taylor did not respect foot binding. Why were some traditions all right with him and others not?

Can you think of traditions you've heard or read about that make you feel uncomfortable or confused? Does that make those traditions wrong? How would you know the difference between a tradition or way of behaving that was wrong and one that was just very different?

ACTIVITIES

HIS 1; SS/FW 2; LIT/LA 3

Lesson Five

Chapter 8: The Tomb of the Living Dead
Chapter 9: Betrayed in the Walled City

PRAISE AND PRAYER: BETRAYAL VERSUS LOYALTY

In chapter 9 of *Shanghaied to China*, Neil Thompson did a terrible thing. **Read Luke 22:4–6.** In what ways were Judas and Neil alike? **Contrast Proverbs 18:24 and Deuteronomy 31:6.** What kind of friend is the Lord God?

Thought: A true friend will never betray a friend.

Prayer: Thank you, God, that I can count on you to stand by me, no matter what.

VOCABULARY AND CONCEPTS

grimaced, stubble, pagoda, incense, gongs, betrayal
What does "common people" on page 88 mean?
What is meant by "halting Chinese" on page 90?

BACKGROUND

During the years of the Taiping revolt, whole regions of the country became battlegrounds. One day rebels controlled a city. The next, Imperial government troops would win a battle, and the city would be theirs. The common people suffered no matter who was in control.

In 1854, most Chinese people followed the *philosophy* of Confucianism. Their *religion* was sometimes Buddhism, Taoism, or "animism," the worship of nature, local gods, ancestors, or idols.

The philosophy of Confucianism was based on good ideas. For example, the philosopher Confucius taught that to live harmoniously required kindness, honesty, and obedience to government. From harmonious families, peaceful villages would grow. Peaceful villages would produce a prosperous nation.

Hudson Taylor's goal to reach inland China was ambitious. Even today a missionary traveling by airplane and train can spend three *days* making the trip from Shanghai to the Xinjiang region. Most missionaries lived in cities like Shanghai but rarely traveled inland. Hudson Taylor wanted to reach those millions of people who had never heard the Gospel.

"For many years he has had no contact with other humans, so he cannot have sinned against anyone."

TALK ABOUT IT

Imagine someone living behind a brick wall to escape sin (see page 96)! Long ago some Christians lived alone in desert caves or in *cloisters* to avoid sin. Even today some people try to escape sin by surrounding themselves *only* with other Christians. Read Romans 7:18–19. Talk together about what you do to try to avoid sin. In what ways are you successful? How are you not successful?

ACTIVITIES

GEO 2; HIS 2; SS/FW 3, 4; LIT/LA 4; CT 1

Lesson Six

Chapter 10: The Long Road Back
Chapter 11: Tornado Lovers

PRAISE AND PRAYER: FORGIVING AND BEING FORGIVEN

In *Shanghaied to China*, Neil Thompson had a hard time believing Hudson Taylor really forgave him. **Read Matthew 6:14–15 and Mark 11:25.** Why do you think Hudson Taylor was willing to forgive Neil? Why is it important to forgive someone if he or she does something wrong to us?

Thought: If we want God to forgive us, we must be willing to forgive others.

Prayer: O God, when I am having a hard time forgiving someone, help me to remember how much you have forgiven me.

VOCABULARY AND CONCEPTS

rousel, malaria, sedan chair (see page 121), waterspout, eerie, fiancée
On page 113 we read "people *milled around.*" What does that mean?
Neil "hailed" a sedan chair. What does that mean?

BACKGROUND

Hudson Taylor and Maria Dyer wanted to get to know each other, but Miss Aldersey, head of the girls' school where Maria taught, would not permit it. In 1854, relationships were not as they are today. No gentleman would visit or talk alone with a young woman. A young woman would be considered wild and improper if she spoke with a man alone. Even an adult woman could not marry without the consent of her father or legal guardian. Miss Dyer's parents were dead, and her legal guardian lived thousands of miles away in England. So Miss Aldersey considered it her responsibility to make sure young Miss Dyer did not do anything so foolish as to take up with the radical Hudson Taylor!

Maria Dyer may not have dared to disobey Miss Aldersey, but she wasn't a helpless person at all! She traveled thousands of miles to dangerous places and taught Chinese women about Jesus. She raised children far from the comforts of England. She watched a child die of cholera and, on more than one occasion, feared her husband would die of overwork and poor health. Like many women in the 1800s, Maria Dyer appeared shy and reserved on the outside because society required it, but on the inside, she had an iron-strong faith, a willingness to work long and hard, and a desire to follow God wherever He led.

For the next few days, I stayed with Namu, helping to care for the wounded and homeless.

TALK ABOUT IT

See pages 120 and 121. Neil's friend Namu says, "They [the Europeans] look at us without really seeing us. It is not honorable. . . ." Have you ever felt someone was looking at you but not really *seeing* you? Share about that experience.

ACTIVITIES

GEO 3; SS/FW 5; LIT/LA 5

Lesson Seven

Chapter 12: Passage on the *Geelong*
More About Hudson Taylor

PRAISE AND PRAYER: GOD'S FORGIVENESS

In the last chapter of *Shanghaied*, how did Hudson Taylor show Neil that he was truly forgiven? How did Neil feel when he accepted Taylor's forgiveness? **Read Psalm 103:11–12 and Luke 7:36–50.** What does God do with our sins when we ask for forgiveness? How did the "sinful woman" in Luke 7 show her love for Jesus? Why? (See v. 47.)

Thought: When we realize that God forgives us because of his great love for us, we cannot help but love him.

Prayer: O God, thank you so much for forgiving my sins! I love you, Lord.

VOCABULARY AND CONCEPTS

situated, grim, primarily

BACKGROUND

The postscript to Chapter 12 tells more about Hudson Taylor's life. Historians know life was hard for this man and his family. The Taylors lost a child to illness. Hudson Taylor's beloved Maria and another child died of cholera in 1870. Even his fellow Christians did not understand or appreciate Hudson Taylor's radical behavior. Dressing and living as a Chinese person made no sense to most missionaries.

Then he grabbed Maria around the waist and kissed her.

Also, Hudson Taylor caused a great uproar in England by recruiting single women as missionaries. Some Christians said only married women should serve with their husbands. While people in England argued about whether it was appropriate for single women to be missionaries, Hudson Taylor brought woman after woman to China. As a result, many Chinese women heard about Jesus who may never have been permitted to listen to male preachers.

Trailblazer authors Dave and Neta Jackson include interesting information about Hudson Taylor on their Web site www.trailblazerbooks.com. Go online to learn more about China Inland Mission, the organization Hudson Taylor began. You'll also find a portrait of Taylor and information about his life.

ACTIVITIES

LIT/LA 6, 7; SS/FW 6, 7, 8

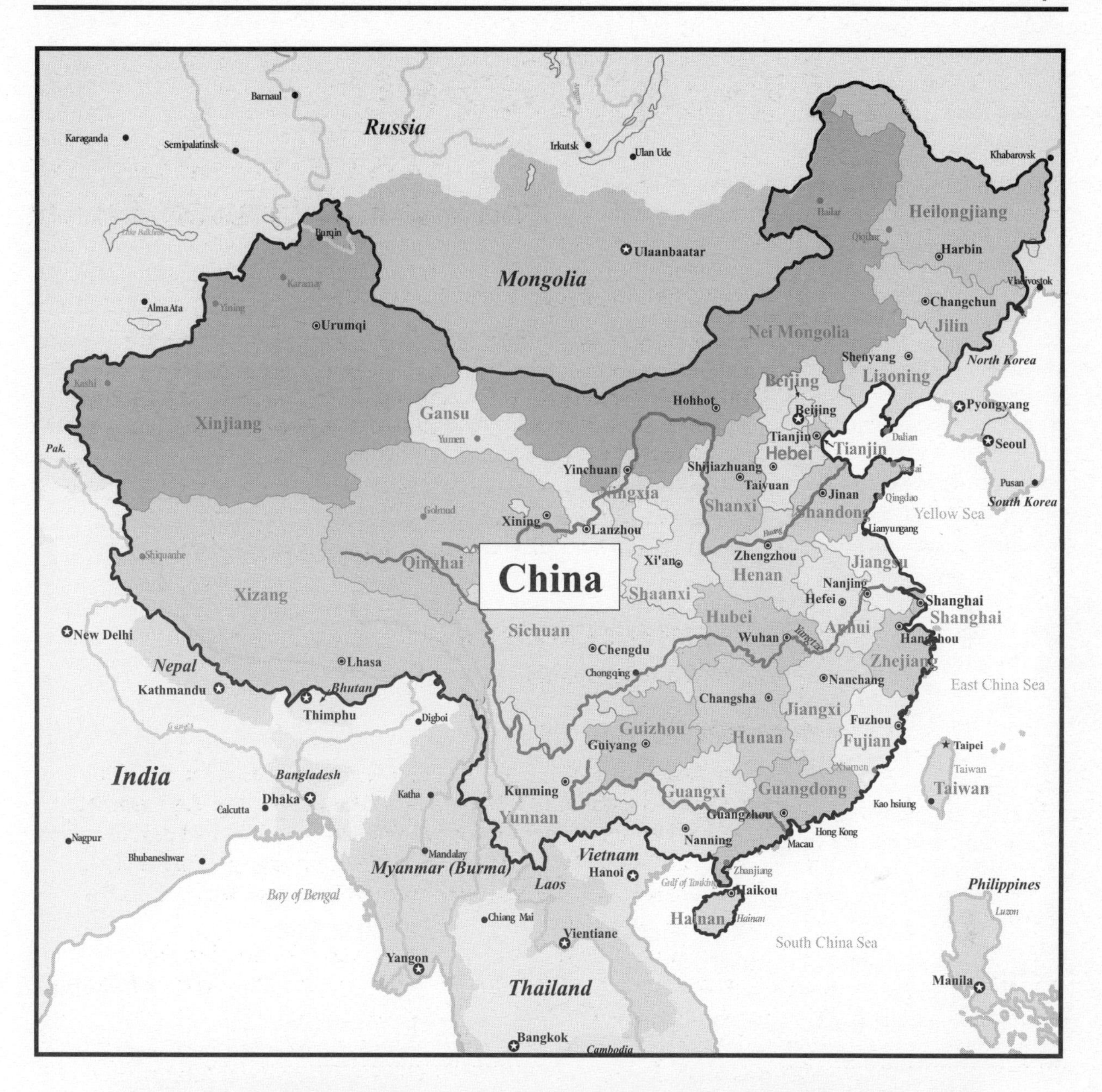
China
Russia
Mongolia
India
Nepal
Bhutan
Bangladesh
Myanmar (Burma)
Laos
Vietnam
Thailand
North Korea
South Korea
Taiwan
Philippines
Pak.
Barnaul
Karaganda
Semipalatinsk
Irkutsk
Ulan Ude
Khabarovsk
Ulaanbaatar
Alma Ata
Urumqi
Heilongjiang
Harbin
Changchun
Jilin
Nei Mongolia
Shenyang
Liaoning
Pyongyang
Seoul
Pusan
Xinjiang
Gansu
Hohhot
Beijing
Tianjin
Hebei
Dalian
Yinchuan
Shijiazhuang
Taiyuan
Jinan
Qingdao
Ningxia
Shanxi
Shandong
Yellow Sea
Xining
Lanzhou
Lianyungang
Qinghai
Xi'an
Zhengzhou
Henan
Jiangsu
Nanjing
Hefei
Shanghai
Xizang
Shaanxi
Hubei
Anhui
New Delhi
Sichuan
Wuhan
Hangzhou
Chengdu
Lhasa
Zhejiang
Kathmandu
Chongqing
Nanchang
East China Sea
Thimphu
Changsha
Jiangxi
Digboi
Guizhou
Hunan
Fuzhou
Guiyang
Fujian
Taipei
Kunming
Guangxi
Guangdong
Katha
Dhaka
Calcutta
Yunnan
Guangzhou
Kao hsiung
Hong Kong
Macau
Nagpur
Nanning
Bhubaneshwar
Mandalay
Hanoi
Zhanjiang
Haikou
Bay of Bengal
Chiang Mai
Hainan
Vientiane
South China Sea
Yangon
Manila
Bangkok

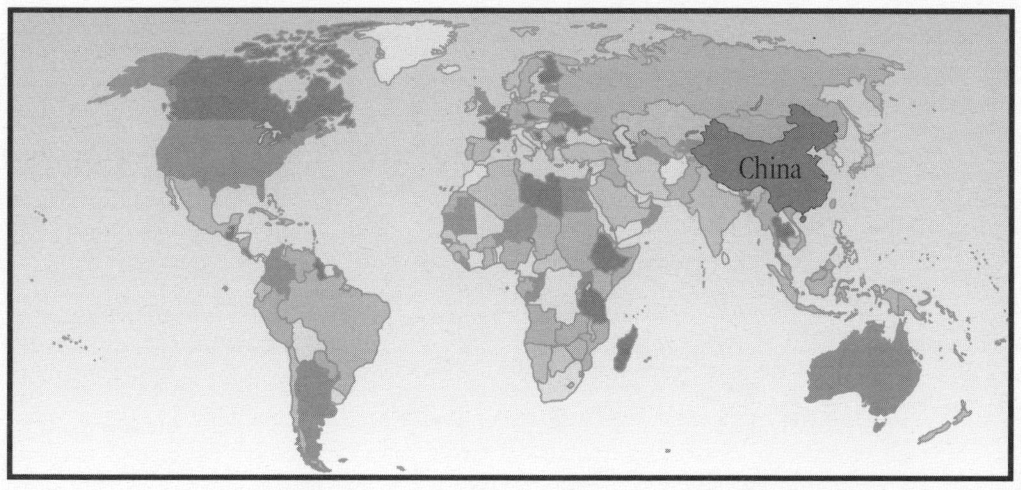
China

Geography

If we know the land, we will know more about the people. In a land like China, with ocean at one border, mountains at another, and one of the world's most desolate deserts in the center, the land determines much about how people live.

As advances in technology (television, Internet, etc.) make our world smaller and smaller, students must know about other countries. To understand the news and politics, students must understand how and where people live around the world. So geography is more than finding China on a map; it is understanding how the land affects people and culture.

GEO 1: Shanghai means "on the water." Find this city on a map. Can you see any geographic reasons why Shanghai would be an important Chinese city? Some historians say Shanghai has always been more "Western" than other Chinese cities. Why might this be? (*Note:* The term "Western" indicates ties or similarities to Europe and America.) (RESEARCH)

GEO 2: Trace a map of China including rivers, deserts, and mountains. Hudson Taylor dreamed of reaching the center of China with the good news of Jesus. What route might he have taken to reach the inland city of Chongqing (sometimes written Ch'ung-ch'ing or Chungking)? Remember, travel in 1854 was overland on foot or by wagon, or on rivers or the ocean by boat. (HANDS-ON)

GEO 3: Could our character Neil really have seen a tornado suck the water from a pond and "spit" it out minutes later? Learn some hair-raising facts about tornadoes from the article "Tornado!" in the June 1987 *National Geographic* magazine. *Tornado* by Jules Archer and *Wild Weather: Tornadoes!* by Lorraine Hopping are two great books about tornadoes. (RESEARCH)

GEO 4: Find the Uyghur (WEE-gur) Autonomous Region on a map (see SS/FW 4). Over the centuries, China conquered, absorbed, and took over other countries and people groups.

One of those countries, Tibet, is a beautiful nation with rich culture and traditions that wishes to be free of Chinese control today. Learn about Tibet at your library in recently published books or online at http://tibet.org or www.nationalgeographic.com (see Resources in this guide). Students can share what they learn about Tibet with their family, class, or homeschool group. (RESEARCH)

GEO 5: Mount Everest is located partly in China and partly in neighboring Nepal. First, find the world's highest mountain on a map or globe. Find its height.

To learn more: Read *The Top of the World* by Steve Jenkins or *To the Top!* by S. A. Kramer. See Mount Everest up close in videos like *Cameramen Who Dared* by National Geographic Videos, *The Making of Everest*, or *Into the Thin Air of Everest, Mountain of Dreams*. (RESEARCH)

GEO 6: View some or all of the following videos about China:

- *The World's Greatest Train Ride*
- *The Great Wall of China*
- *The Silk Road*
- *China: An Open Door*
- *China: A Journey in Pictures*

(VIDEO)

GEO 7: Read *China: The Land* by Bobbie Kalman. This well-written, simple book describes the daily lives and experiences of regular people in China. Color photos and prints of Chinese art. A wonderful read-together book. (READING)

History

An old saying claims that people who don't know history are doomed to repeat it. Whether that is true or not, knowing history helps us to understand why people behave as they do, how governments work, and how one event causes another as history unfolds.

HIS 1: Ask an adult to explain the expression "Politics makes friends of enemies." With this saying in mind, write a short essay explaining why England supported rebel groups like the Red Turbans against the Chinese government. (WRITING)

HIS 2: Why would a city be walled? China has always been one of the largest nations on earth. Defending thousands of miles of borders is a nearly impossible job. Read *The Great Wall* by Elizabeth Mann to learn how the Chinese government once tried to protect its land and people by building a thirty-foot high wall of "rammed earth" thousands of miles across China. This forty-four–page book includes beautiful illustrations and maps as well as grand stories of battles, emperors, and China's history.

To build your own rammed-earth wall you'll need sand, six bricks, a spray bottle of water, and a tool for pounding (a rubber mallet; a flat, smooth stone; or even a can of soup).

- Form two stacks of three bricks each. (Place the wide side on the ground or the bricks will tumble.) Set the two stacks six inches apart, long sides facing each other.
- Mist the sand with water until it is moist but not wet. Scoop sand between the bricks until it is level with the bottom bricks. Pound the sand with your tool until it is packed hard.
- Scoop sand until it is even with the second level of bricks. Pound again. Fill to the top and pound again until the surface is hard to the touch.

Carefully remove the bricks.

You can learn more about rammed-earth construction on the Internet. People still build houses with rammed earth today! (HANDS-ON)

HIS 3: Read Bobbie Kalman's book *China: The People.* Second in a series about China's land, people, and culture, this well-written, accessible book includes photos and artwork. A good read-aloud.

Discuss the following: What do you notice about the photos of children in this book? Did you know one-fifth of the people in the world live in China? Why do you think the Chinese government has such strict rules limiting the number of children in a family? Do you think this is a good idea? On page 24 of *China: The People*, the author writes that, until recently, all Chinese workers doing the same job were paid the same. Doing more or better work didn't mean more pay. What do you think of this? (READING)

HIS 4: Check your library for books about China's history. Picture books like *Ancient China* by Brian Williams include photos and illustrations and offer relevant information without excessive detail. (RESEARCH)

HIS 5: Read about the philosopher Confucius and write a few paragraphs about him. When did he live? What did he teach? Why is that important, even today, in China? (WRITING)

HIS 6: In Hudson Taylor's time, an emperor ruled China. This man was all-powerful. He did not earn his job, but inherited it from his father. The emperor and other nobles believed the gods had given them power as a reward for the goodness of their ancestors.

Common people had no power or rights. They struggled to survive. They paid high taxes so the rulers could live in luxury. Laws were created by and for the rulers and the rich. As the old saying goes, absolute power led to absolute corruption. Corruption led to protest. Protest led to war.

In 1911, a revolution finally ended thousands of years of Imperial (emperor) rule. But then the Chinese people had to learn to govern themselves for the first time. How would they do it? Some people had democratic ideas. The military wanted to keep power and control. Russia's experiment with Communism particularly appealed to the poor, who hoped a "people's government" would work for them instead of only for the rich. Today, China's government is Communist.

Assignment: Find out how Communism works in China, and write a short description of Communist beliefs and government. Write a paragraph giving your own opinions about the good and bad qualities of this form of government.

(*Note:* Students may not understand both positive and negative qualities of Communism. For example, government-owned factories are able, if the government chooses, to pay fair wages or offer healthcare to everyone. But if the government does *not* give fair wages or healthcare, people have no place to turn to for help.)

Students interested in government and current events may search online or in an index of periodicals for articles about recent changes in Chinese Communism. (RESEARCH)

HIS 7: Read *A Boy's War* by David Michell, a fascinating, true story of the children of missionaries to China who spent the six years of World War II in a Japanese concentration camp. This book is published by Overseas Missionary Fellowship, which began as China Inland Mission, the organization Hudson Taylor began in 1865. (READING)

HIS 8: We say missionaries go "overseas." Find out how difficult that truly was in 1854, when Hudson Taylor traveled to China, by learning about clipper ships. Good titles include *Sailing Ships* by Thomas Bayley, *Ships and Other Seacraft* by Brian Williams, and *The Visual Dictionary of Ships and Sailing*. *Tall Ships* by Kathryn Lasky even has actual photos of a storm at sea! (RESEARCH)

HIS 9: Cover your walls with sailing ships! Dover Publications offers two historically accurate coloring books, *Historic Sailing Ships* and *American Sailing Ships*, with examples of clipper ships similar to the *Dumfries.* (HANDS-ON)

HIS 10: Check your local newspaper every day or look at recent issues of news magazines like *Time*, *Newsweek*, or *U.S. News and World Report* and clip articles about China. Read and share what you find with your family, class, or homeschool group. (RESEARCH)

HIS 11: Older students: **Read *China Cry* by Nora Lam. This true story tells how a Christian woman was able to leave Communist China. Younger students: *Read *Escape by Night*, a true story of a family's escape from Communist China. (READING)

HIS 12: TRAILBLAZERS online!

Visit www.trailblazerbooks.com to find Dave and Neta Jackson's TRAILBLAZERS Web site. Click on the **cover** of *Shanghaied to China* to find information about Hudson Taylor. Click on **Web Links** to see a portrait of Hudson Taylor, an article about his life from *Christian History* magazine, and a short biographical sketch. Also, check out the timeline and maps. (RESEARCH)

HIS 13: **View *Inn of the Sixth Happiness* about Gladys Aylward, a missionary who saved children in China during World War II. (It is available for rental as well as on interlibrary loan.) The themes and issues in this film are not appropriate for younger children. The story can also be found in books or in the TRAILBLAZER BOOK *Flight of the Fugitives.* (VIDEO)

HIS 14: Jean Fritz, author of many good books about history for young readers, grew up in China as a child of missionaries. Read *Homesick: My Own Story,* Jean Fritz's own words about growing up in 1940s China. (READING)

HIS 15: View the National Geographic video *Dinosaur Hunters*. This film follows the expedition of archeologists in China. (VIDEO)

HIS 16: See these *National Geographic* articles about China:

- "China's Warriors Rise from the Earth" (October 1996) An army of life-size terra-cotta warrior figures are forced to honor an ancient emperor. Amazing photos.
- "Lord of the Mongols: Genghis Khan" (December 1996)
- "Xinjaing" (March 1996) An article about minority cultures including the Uyghurs.
- "China's Buddhist Caves" (April 1996) Cave paintings and art.
- "Silk Road's Lost World" (March 1996) The route followed by silk caravans.
- "Journey to China's Far West" (March 1980) China's minority cultures. Good photos.

(READING)

HIS 17: In ancient times Chinese culture and science advanced far beyond that of other nations. While much of Europe still believed demons and "vapors" caused disease, the Chinese practiced herbal medicine and acupuncture. Today, Western medical doctors are learning acupuncture techniques used a thousand years ago in China.

Many important discoveries and inventions were made by the Chinese people. In fact, China was first to discover gunpowder, paper, printing, the compass, the abacus, and silk making. Assign students to investigate the history of one of these inventions and present a short report to the class, co-op group, or family. (WRITING)

Social Studies and Folkways

Folkways are the traditions of a people and culture. Art, food, storytelling, music, dance, drama, literature, and even religion are mirrors reflecting the heart and soul of a nation and its people. Learning about folkways helps us understand people and their customs.

For Western people, understanding Asian culture, values, and traditions is especially challenging. Our cultures are very, very different. Yet, as Hudson Taylor discovered when he willingly gave up his British ways to adopt Chinese clothing, traditions, and life-style, when we share the traditions of our neighbors, they become friends.

SS/FW 1: What is a junk? Check *The Visual Dictionary of Ships and Sailing*. Make special note of the sails! Photos of junks can be found in issues of *National Geographic* magazine or books. Read *The Story About Ping*, which is set on a junk on the Yangtze River in China, to a younger child. (RESEARCH)

SS/FW 2: Even today, ethnic groups in China wear different traditional clothes. Look in books and encyclopedias, on the Internet, or in old issues of *National Geographic* or other magazines for photos of traditional clothing. Cut or copy pictures to create a poster with a map of China showing traditional clothing and the region of China where each is worn. (HANDS-ON)

SS/FW 3: Learn about Confucianism, Buddhism, or Taoism. The resource list at the end of this guide lists some books. You will find others in your library. Write a short report telling about the beliefs, practices, and traditions of people who follow this religion or philosophy. (WRITING)

SS/FW 4: Enjoy photos and stories about culture and traditions as you read about the people groups of inland China today in *National Geographic* magazine:

- "Xinjaing" (March 1996) Uyghur people (also spelled *Uygur* or *Uygher*)
- "Journey to China's Far West" (March 1980)
- "The Silk Road's Lost World" (March 1996)
- "Genghis Khan" (December 1996) Mongolian people

A class or homeschool group might divide these articles so each person can read and share about one people group in China today. Back issues of *National Geographic* can be found in libraries or ordered at (800) 777-2800. Cost is $5 per issue. (SPEECH)

SS/FW 5: Rice is very important in Asia. In fact, the word *rice* is used in some dialects to mean "meal." Here is a recipe for fried rice students can prepare themselves:

Ingredients: 3 cups cooked rice; 3 tablespoons oil (peanut oil is especially good); 1 beaten egg; 1/4 cup chopped green onions; 1/2 cup chopped fresh mushrooms; 1/2 cup frozen or fresh peas; 1/4 cup grated carrots; soy sauce; and pepper. (Optional: 1 cup cooked chicken, beef, pork, or shrimp. Ginger and garlic can be added to the hot oil.)

1. Heat oil in wok or frying pan.
2. Pour in beaten egg and stir-fry until scrambled.
3. Add green onions, mushrooms, peas, and carrots. Stir-fry.
4. Add cooked rice and pepper.
5. Stir-fry until rice turns brown.
6. Remove from heat. Add *small* amount of soy sauce. Stir.
7. Enjoy!

(COOKING)

SS/FW 6: *"Ni hao"* (NEE-how) means "Hello." Hudson Taylor studied Mandarin Chinese in college. You don't have to wait that long! Your public library will have access to tapes of spoken Chinese. Listen to the rhythm and tones. Try to imitate some words. You may find it difficult to duplicate some of the sounds in spoken Chinese just as Chinese people find some sounds in English difficult. Learn some words and phrases to teach your family, class, or homeschool group. (RESEARCH)

SS/FW 7: Of course, speaking Chinese wouldn't have been enough for a missionary like Hudson Taylor. He had to write Chinese characters, as well. The Chinese language does not have phonetic letters, but symbolic "characters."

At the library, look for books like *Long Is a Dragon: Chinese Writing for Children* by Peggy Goldstein, *The Chinese Word for Horse and Other Stories* by John Lewis, or two storybooks by Huy Voun Lee, *In the Park* and *At the Beach.* You'll find examples of Chinese writing and learn how these interesting characters were invented and what they mean.

For this activity, large sheets of butcher paper or newsprint are nice to work with. Using narrow paintbrushes and black tempera paint, make a mural of Chinese characters. Below each character be sure to write or illustrate its meaning. You'll discover some Chinese characters look like the word they communicate. (HANDS-ON)

SS/FW 8: View the video version of *The Chinese Word for Horse*. Copy Chinese characters, pausing the video or rewinding to watch Chinese writers draw each character. (VIDEO)

SS/FW 9: Food! Mandarin, Hunan, Szechwan...Chinese cooking is as diverse as its people. In some places a good cook is called a "doctor of food," and friends wish one another good luck by saying, "May you eat today," or "Good fortune comes into your mouth."

Explore Chinese cooking by doing one of the following:

- Ask to visit a Chinese restaurant in your community. Schedule a visit during a slow period—probably early morning—to watch cooks prepare food and listen to them describe how they learned to cook, the type of Chinese cuisine they prepare, and how their own family came to America. After the kitchen visit, be sure to stay for lunch.
- Plan a library trip to check out cookbooks of different types of Chinese cooking. Choose one dish from each type and plan and prepare a celebration dinner. The whole family can chop vegetables, stir-fry foods, and enjoy the meal. Chinese cooks often choose spicy and mild foods or hot and cold foods to create *balance.* Confucius taught that balance in all things is important, and even Chinese cooks apply the principle to their food!
- Visit a Chinese or Asian market in your area. Good prepared sauces can be found in markets often located near multi-national university communities. The smells and package labels will be new and fascinating. Try preparing a simple soup mix—but don't forget all the directions will be written in Chinese characters!

You also may find inexpensive paper lanterns or chopsticks to use for your celebration meal. Be sure to purchase oolong, bancha, or another oriental tea. Traditional Chinese preparation requires boiling water be poured over loose leaves in a pot or cup. After the tea is brewed, remove the leaves with a wire strainer or allow them to sink to the bottom of the cup. (HANDS-ON)

SS/FW 10: Decorate your celebration table with traditional paper lanterns. Library books will describe many different styles. A simple lantern can be constructed from heavy art or watercolor paper (watercolor paper is beautiful for this project). Ball-shaped lanterns are easily made by gluing one-inch strips of paper at the top and bottom with multicolored pieces of opaque tissue paper between the strips.

To make a box-shaped lantern, fold rectangular art or watercolor paper into quarters along its width. Snowflake-like shapes cut along the folds create openings for candlelight. Colored tissue paper can be glued to cover the cut shapes.

Lanterns may be lit using candles. For safety, votive or tea candles may be placed inside a small glass jar with at least three inches between the top of the candle flame and the sides of the lantern. (HANDS-ON)

SS/FW 11: Chinese paper-cutting is an old and beautiful tradition. You'll need sharp scissors, tracing paper, pencils, and good quality art or watercolor paper. Older children may use precision knives with supervision. Check your library for patterns. Whole books are written about paper-cutting for children and adults. The video *Chinese Paper-Cuts* shows how to create lovely artwork with nothing but scissors and paper. This video is especially interesting because students can pause it and trace intricate paper-cut patterns right from the TV screen using tracing paper. (HANDS-ON)

SS/FW 12: Jean Fritz, author of numerous books about history for young readers, grew up in China as a child of missionaries. Read her own story about growing up in 1940s China, *Homesick: My Own Story*. The book is also suggested in HIS 14, but readers will learn much about the traditions and daily lives of Chinese people from the viewpoint of someone like themselves—an American child. (READING)

SS/FW 13: Who hasn't seen photos or film footage of Chinese New Year celebrations complete with men in dragon masks dancing or children flying dragon kites? People also wear lion masks. In some regions of China, dragons are symbols of power and strength. In other regions, dragons are symbols of Satan. For that reason, directions for a lion mask are included here:

You'll need one box larger than your head for the lion's head and another smaller box, about the size of a shoebox, for its snout. Using a staple gun, or brass brads and a hole-punch tool, connect the boxes.

Paint the boxes golden brown.

Cut eyes from construction paper. Draw mouth with marker or paint. Insert broom straws or toothpicks as whiskers. Cut and curl strips of gold, yellow, and brown paper, then glue the strips around the lion's head for a mane. Staple long strips of brown and gold cloth to the top and sides of the lion's head. The mask fits over a person's head, and the strips of cloth move as the person dances and moves with music and rhythm instruments. Chinese celebrators wear lion and dragon costumes in parades.

This mask/costume can also be made in miniature to be used as a hand puppet. Follow the above directions using smaller boxes.

Chinese mask makers also shape the head from papier-mâché. (HANDS-ON)

SS/FW 14: Read "China's Warriors Rise From the Earth" in the October 1996 issue of *National Geographic*. This article shows readers a great deal about Chinese attitudes toward royalty, death, and honor. It is also a fascinating look at the use of art. (READING)

SS/FW 15: A good read-aloud is *China: The Culture* by Bobbie Kalman. In short sections with attractive photos and illustrations, Kalman tells about Chinese art, theater, food, traditions, festivals, and games. (READING)

SS/FW 16: Learn about Buddhism, the religion practiced by many Chinese in Hudson Taylor's time. A simple book like *I Am a Buddhist* by Daniel Quinn will give basic explanatory information. The goal of this activity is to simply understand the Buddhist view of the world, deities, and human life and experience. Ask students to write a one-page paper describing Buddhism.

(*Note:* In exposing students to non-Christian religions, one challenge is to communicate respect for other people and cultures while acknowledging the truth that only Jesus offers salvation and the way to God. Words like *heathen* or *pagan* can be dismissive and fail to acknowledge that people following other religions often *want* to be right with God, yet cannot find Him. Hudson Taylor understood people who honestly wanted to find God and be holy, but without Jesus were always trying and always failing to earn their way to God, perfection, and heaven.

Understanding is more than knowing why Jesus is God and Buddha isn't. Understanding leads to compassion and a missionary's heart. Understanding reveals the great, undeserved gift of forgiveness in Christ in contrast to the fear and uncertainty resulting from a works-based religious philosophy like Buddhism.)
(WRITING)

Literature and Language Arts

Stories are windows to understanding people and their culture. When we enjoy folktales or listen to song lyrics from another culture, we see and appreciate the creativity of the people.

Reading books set in another culture, like *Shanghaied to China,* also makes us better writers. We see how words are used to tell a story, describe a scene, or reveal a character. Students can experiment, using those techniques in their own writing.

LIT/LA 1: Storm at Sea!

The sea was really rolling by this time. The water was as dark as gray slate with lacy patterns of foam stretched over its surface. The clouds that had towered like snow-capped mountains when I had first seen them were now upon us, hanging low, their dark bellies almost dragging across the crests of the waves (pages 21–22).

In this passage we look out from the deck of the *Dumfries* and see the storm coming in across

the Irish Channel. Imagine yourself watching a storm approach. Describe the scene as you see it. Where are you? Perhaps hiking in the mountains? On the top floor of a skyscraper in Chicago? In a tent in the forest? In a small airplane far from the airport? On the prairie in Kansas? In the outfield of a baseball diamond?

What do you see? What are your emotions? What physical feelings happen in your body as you watch the clouds gather and turn from gray to black until the sun disappears? (WRITING)

LIT /LA 2: Note the "sayings" or proverbs in chapter 3. How might sayings help sailors remember important information? Interview people you know until you can find at least five sayings that give information. For example, "A penny saved is a penny earned" teaches thrift, but it doesn't give information about how to save. On the other hand, an old saying of American pioneer farmers, "One [seed] for the farmer, one for the crow, one for the dry month, one for the row," told farmers to plant two seeds for every plant they hoped to harvest because drought and crows would get the rest. Share the sayings you find with your family or home-school group. (SPEECH)

LIT/LA 3: Where did the word *spinster* come from? What does it mean now? Look in a dictionary to find words that once had very different meanings than they do today. Can you think of some words that are newly invented in our culture? (*Note:* The evolving language of technology offers a wealth of possibilities for this exercise.) Make a list of what you find. (RESEARCH)

LIT/LA 4:

> I just lay where I had fallen and cried and slept and cried until morning. . . . I was a robber and had been robbed. I had been betrayed and was, in turn, betrayed (page 108).

Here Neil faces the truth that he has betrayed his friend. Write a sketch of a scene where, in order to reach a goal, receive recognition, or achieve some accomplishment, someone betrays a friend. At first the friend doesn't realize she or he has been betrayed. Then, in a split second, the truth becomes clear. Create a single scene beginning at that exact moment. Don't tell your readers what the betrayal was or what will happen next; just let your readers feel and experience the moment when the friend realizes she or he has been betrayed and the betrayer knows his or her betrayal has been discovered.

Choose either the betrayer or the friend as your main character and write from that main character's point of view. Close your eyes and picture the scene: Where are your characters? (In a restaurant? At school? Alone in a field? Seeing each other in a crowd?) What do their faces look like? What does your main character see? Think? Feel? Do? Say? Does your main character hear sounds? See his or her surroundings?

Writing tip: A writer uses the main character's feelings, thoughts, and words to let the reader experience what is happening. *Telling* is not enough. A good writer *shows* what happens with description. Think of your writing as a camera that not only shows what can be seen, but what the main character is feeling and thinking, as well. (WRITING)

LIT/LA 5: See pages 120 and 121. Neil's friend Namu says, "They [the Europeans] look at us without really seeing us. It is not honorable."

A social worker once wanted to understand how elderly people were treated. She dressed like an elderly woman and wore a gray-haired wig and makeup, but her disguise wasn't very good. Anyone who looked closely would have realized she was only pretending to be old. Amazingly, although she went around the city dressed as an elderly person for weeks, *no one* noticed! No one noticed because no one really *saw.*

Are there people you look at but don't really *see*? How do you feel realizing this? Write an essay telling your experiences, feelings, and thoughts about this. (WRITING)

LIT/LA 6: Here's a beautiful word picture from *Shanghaied to China*:

> Early in the morning, as a timid grayness crept into the eastern sky, I got out of bed and tiptoed out into the cold March air. For the last time I walked the streets of Shanghai dressed as a Chinese boy (page 137).

Close your eyes and picture "timid grayness." How does it creep "into the eastern sky"? Isn't this just a fancy way of saying night was over but the sun hadn't risen? The authors *show* us an image of morning light "creeping" into the sky, turning the world from black to gray just a little bit at a time instead of just *telling* us that morning was coming. Why did they do this?

Choose a scene in nature—perhaps a sunrise or sunset, the trees and sky just before a big storm, early morning after a snowfall, midnight in the woods, or "old" snow in the city in late winter. Imagine yourself as a camera, seeing and recording every detail. See the shapes and colors. Smell the air. Touch. Listen. Make a list of describing words that come to mind.

Your assignment is to "paint" a word picture of one to three paragraphs. Don't just *tell* your readers about this scene; use your words to *show* it. (WRITING)

LIT/LA 7: Youth With a Mission (YWAM) sends young people all over the globe to "soften the spiritual ground" by praying, share about Jesus by preaching and speaking, and show the love of God by serving. YWAM has also published a new biography of Hudson Taylor, *Hudson Taylor: Deep in the Heart of China,* by Janet and Geoff Benge. You can order this book at (800) 922-2143 ($8.99 plus $3 shipping).

This great organization publishes other books about missions. Ask for their catalog. They offer a discount for quantity orders to homeschoolers and Christian schools. (READING)

LIT/LA 8: Request the book *Multicultural Plays for Children* by Pamela Gerke from your library or find another collection of international scripts for young performers. Gerke includes a script for "Ma Lien and the Magic Paintbrush," a traditional Chinese folktale.

Although the script suggests detailed backdrops, a single countryside scene to create atmosphere will work just as well. Costuming is very simple. Younger children might enjoy creating simple costumes and portraying the animal characters that have no lines.

Consider having your co-op group or class perform "Ma Lien and the Magic Paintbrush" for a nearby nursery school, a play group, or younger family members. (DRAMA)

LIT/LA 9: Collections of Chinese folktales abound in libraries and bookstores. Assign students to read, learn, and *tell* one folktale to a homeschool group or class. Storytelling is a traditional Chinese art form. In fact, most folktales were *told* for hundreds of years before they were written.

Storytelling is challenging and fun. Students read and re-read a story until they know it. Some students benefit from writing the story out in their own words, then memorizing the story to tell. Other students want to memorize the story as written and recite it word-for-word. Still other students will "digest" the story and make it their own, telling it in a flow of their own words and the writer's words.

Storytelling comes alive when tellers create voices for characters, use sound effects, dramatic gestures and intonation, and draw the audience in with eye contact, voice, and words.

If students are attracted to storytelling, listening to tapes of skilled tellers will expose them to techniques that make even simple stories come alive. Jay O'Callahan, Jackie Torrence, David Holt, and Syd Lieberman are just a few of the many nationally known storytellers whose stories are available on tape at most libraries or on interlibrary loan. (DRAMA)

LIT/LA 10: Read a Chinese folktale. Assign students to write it in their own words and illustrate the story. Create a folktale display in your classroom or home. (WRITING)

LIT/LA 11: Read folktales like *The Seven Chinese Brothers, Tikki Tikki Tembo,* or *Ping* aloud to younger children. (READING)

LIT/LA 12: Proverbs or mottoes are common in Chinese culture. Read these aloud and ask students to guess what they might mean:

- We know how to eat bitterness. (We can hold up in hard times.)
- The rice is cooked. (What's done is done.)
- The fox cannot hide its tail. (True character will show sooner or later.)
- Come and eat rice. (You're invited for dinner!)
- Try to fish the moon from the bottom of the sea. (Reach for the impossible.)
- He measures the sea with an oyster shell. (His understanding is shallow….He doesn't know what he's talking about.)
- Plug your ears while you steal the bell. (You're deceiving yourself.)
- Dripping water will wear through the rock. (Keep trying. You succeed little by little.)
- The gruel is thin, and the monks are many. (There's not enough to go around. Times are hard.)

Find some wise sayings from the Old Testament book of Proverbs. Assign students to read a few proverbs aloud and tell what they mean.

OR

Assign students to create and write three proverbs of their own. Remember, proverbs aren't rules declaring "do this, don't do that"; they use a symbol or image to illustrate a principle of life. Try working together on the first proverb, asking for and writing down suggestions from everyone. Then release students to create their own.

During Hudson Taylor's time, proverbs were stitched onto cloth and framed for display in the home. Ask students to write and illustrate their proverbs for display. (HANDS-ON)

The Church Today

Of course, reaching China for Christ didn't stop with Hudson Taylor. Today, missionaries are not welcomed by the Communist government, but Christians bring the good news of Jesus to China in other ways. They travel, study in universities, and even live and operate businesses in China. These missionaries live, as Hudson Taylor did, with and like their Chinese neighbors. Sometimes women show respect for Muslim culture by covering their heads, and children attend Chinese schools.

MEGA PROJECT IDEA

Many missionaries have a special desire to travel where no one has ever said or heard the name of Jesus. God puts a special group of people on a missionary's heart. Hudson Taylor wanted to reach central China, a huge territory, then unmapped and mostly unexplored by Europeans. David Livingstone went to places in Africa where no European person had ever been. Nate Saint and Jim Elliot prayed for the Auca people in South America to know Jesus as their Savior.

Even today, whole groups of people have not heard about Jesus. Homeschooling families or classes in a Christian school can take a group of people into their hearts to learn about and pray for.

One "people group," the Uyghur people in northern China, have had few opportunities to hear about Jesus. Most Uyghurs are Muslim; only a handful are Christian. There are no churches. People are afraid to become Christians because the government persecutes believers. People who accept Christ are rejected by their families and friends. They may lose their jobs or be threatened physically. A woman could be divorced by her husband or a child thrown out of his or her home.

Like Hudson Taylor, who wanted to reach central China, students can take the Uyghur people into their hearts. Here are ways to be part of reaching these people with the good news that Jesus loves them:

CT 1: Make a poster:

Read about the Uyghur people (also spelled *Uighur, Uygur,* or *Uygher*) in the March 1996 issue of *National Geographic* magazine. You may wish to purchase your own issue so you can cut out the pictures to create a prayer poster. Trace a map of China on posterboard and mount the photos of Uyghur people around the edge. Note Kashgar and Urumchi, main cities in Uyghur territory. (HANDS-ON)

CT 2: Learn about the history, culture, and daily lives of Uyghur people. Write a report to share with your co-op group, family, or class. (WRITING)

Online resources about the Uyghur people:

www.encarta.com/ewa/pages/a/47590.htm (maps)

www.encarta.com/ewa/pages/a/36980.htm (music)

www.chinavista.com/experience/ (dance)

www.ping.be/travelspot/china.htm (history and photos)

www1.kcn.ne.jp/~narikawa/english.htm (photos, see Xinjaing page)

www.antioch.com.sg/mission/asianmo/profiles.html (missions to the Uyghurs)

Other resources:

Contact RUN Ministries (Reaching Uyghurs Now) at P.O. Box 6543, Virginia Beach, VA 23456; by email 102047.2422@compuserve.com; or by phone at (757) 427-9089. RUN provides resources for prayer groups, mission agencies, individuals, and churches about outreach to the Uyghur people. RUN provides:

- **Prayer resources**: six-sided prayer card or thirty-one–day prayer booklet featuring cultural, historical, and spiritual information about Uyghurs and daily prayer points.
- **Videos:** *An Oasis in the Desert* and *From Sweden to Xinjiang: Caravans of Hope* (history of Uyghur missions).
- **Audiotapes:** tapes of Uyghur worship services and music.

Donations are requested to cover the costs of these materials. (RESEARCH)

CT 3: Commit yourselves and your family to pray for the Uyghur people. Bethany World Prayer Center has information for praying at the following Web site:

www.bethany.com/profiles/p_code1/912.html

Pray for teams of missionaries now in Uyghur cities. Pray for the tiny gathering of Uyghur people who meet secretly to worship. Pray for U.S. Christian students who participate each summer in a university cultural exchange program. Pray for the Uyghur students who will hear about Jesus for the first time. (PRAYER)

CT 4: View the twenty-eight–minute film *Rebeka Goes to China*, the story of a Christian child living in China today. This and other child-appropriate mission-oriented videos and posters are available from the Mennonite Central Committee. Contact the MCC resource library at (717) 859-1151 for a catalog or rental information. Rental costs are minimal, often only postage. (VIDEO)

Resources

Titles in bold indicate resources particularly recommended for supplementing this Curriculum Guide.

Online: The following Internet Web sites are mentioned in this guide:

- **www.antioch.com.sg/mission/asianmo/profiles.html** (missions to the Uyghurs)
- www.chinavista.com/experience/ (dance)
- www.encarta.com/ewa/pages/a/47590.htm (maps)
- www.encarta.com/ewa/pages/a/36980.htm (music)
- www1.kcn.ne.jp/~narikawa/english/htm (photos, see Xinjaing page)
- www.nationalgeographic.com
- www.ping.be/travelspot/china.htm (history and photos)
- www.sh.com/culture/legend/legend.htm (folktales)
- http://tibet.org
- www.trailblazerbooks.com

Print: The following resources are mentioned in this guide:

American Sailing Ships. Chicago: Dover (historically accurate coloring book)

Ancient China (A See Through History Book) by Brian Williams. New York: Viking, 1996.

At the Beach by Huy Voun Lee. New York: Holt, 1994.

A Boy's War by David Michell. Wheaton, IL: Overseas Missionary Fellowship, 1988.

China Cry by Nora Lam. Nashville: Thomas Nelson, 1991.

China: The People by Bobbie Kalman. New York: Crabtree, 1989.

China: The Land by Bobbie Kalman. New York: Crabtree, 1990.

China: The Culture by Bobbie Kalman. New York: Crabtree, 1990.

The Chinese Word for Horse and Other Stories by John Lewis. New York: Schocken Books, 1980.

Escape by Night. Crossroads Publications, 1998. (408) 378-6658.

Flight of the Fugitives by Dave and Neta Jackson. Minneapolis: Bethany House, 1994.

From Slave Ship to Freedom Road by Julius Lester. New York: Dial, 1998.

The Great Wall by Elizabeth Mann. San Francisco: Mikaya Press, 1997.

Historic Sailing Ships. Chicago: Dover. (historically accurate coloring book)

Homesick: My Own Story by Jean Fritz. New York: Dell, 1984.

Hudson Taylor: Deep in the Heart of China by Janet and Geoff Benge. Seattle: YWAM, 1998. (800) 922-2143

I Am a Buddhist by Daniel Quinn. New York: Rosen Publishing, 1997.

In the Park by Huy Voun Lee. New York: Holt, 1998.

Long Is a Dragon: Chinese Writing for Children by Peggy Goldstein. Berkeley, CA: Pacific View Press, 1991.

Multicultural Plays for Children by Pamela Gerke. Lyme, NH: Smit and Kraus, 1996.

National Geographic. Washington, D.C.: National Geographic Society.[1]

The Old China Trade by Francis Carpenter. Boston: Coward, McCann, Geohagen, 1976.

Sailing Ships by Thomas Bayley. New York: Orchard, 1998.

Ships and Other Seacraft by Brian Williams. Toronto: Warwick Press, 1984.

Tall Ships by Kathryn Lasky. New York: Scribner, 1978.

The Story About Ping by Marjorie Flack and Kurt Wiese. New York: Puffin, 1977.

The Top of the World: Climbing Mount Everest by Steve Jenkins. New York: Houghton Mifflin, 1999.

To the Top! by S.A. Kramer. New York: Random House, 1993.

Tornado by Jules Archer. New York:

Crestwood, 1991.
The Visual Dictionary of Ships and Sailing (An Eyewitness Book). New York: DK Publishers, 1991.
Wild Weather: Tornadoes! by Lorraine Hopping. New York: Scholastic, 1994.

Video: The following resources are mentioned in this guide:
Cameramen Who Dared, National Geographic Videos, 1995.
China: A Journey in Pictures, AVG Video Inc., 1986 (Kodak Discover the World Films).
China: An Open Door, AGI Productions, 1997.
Chinese Paper-Cuts, Kwang Hwa Mass Communications, 1991.
The Chinese Word for Horse, Media Guild, 1986.
Dinosaur Hunters, National Geographic Videos, 1997.
From Sweden to Xinjiang: Caravans of Hope, RUN (Reaching Uyghurs Now) Ministries, 1997. P.O. Box 6543, Virginia Beach, VA 23456; (757) 427-9089.
The Great Wall of China, Actuality Productions, 1990.
Inn of the Sixth Happiness, CBS/Fox Films.
Into the Thin Air of Everest, Mountain of Dreams, Goldhil Video, 1997.
The Making of Everest, National Geographic Videos, 1996.
An Oasis in the Desert. RUN Ministries (see citation above).
Rebeka Goes to China, MCC resource library, (717) 859-1151.
The Silk Road, Central Park Media, 1990.
The World's Greatest Train Ride, Publishers' Choice Video, 1995.

[1]Articles and issues of *National Geographic* magazine listed in activity descriptions. Back issues: (800) 647-5463. Education Dept: (800) 368-2728 for additional resources.